Bristol F W9-BGK-762

Bristol Public Library

Make way for the monsters from
MONSTER MANOR

#1 Von Skalpel's Experiment

#2 Frankie Rocks the House

#3 Beatrice's Spells

#4 Wolf Man Stu Bites Back

#5 Horror Gets Slimed

#6 Count Snobula Vamps It Up

#7 Sally Gets Silly

#8 Runaway Zombie!

MONSTER MANOR
Runaway zombie!

by PAUL MARTIN and MANU BOISTEAU
Adapted by LISA PAPADEMETRIOU
Illustrated by MANU BOISTEAU

Hyperion Books for Children
New York

visit us at www.abdopublishing.com

Reinforced library bound edition published in 2012 by Spotlight,
a division of ABDO Publishing Group, 8000 West 78th Street, Edina,
Minnesota 55439. Spotlight produces high-quality reinforced library
bound editions for schools and libraries. This edition reprinted
by arrangement with Disney Book Group, LLC.

Printed in the United States of America, Melrose Park, Illinois.
052011
092011
 This book contains at least 10% recycled materials.

First published under the title *Maudit Manoir, Bonne Nuit
les Zombies!* in France by Bayard Jeunesse. © Bayard Editions
Jeunesse, 2002 Text Copyright © 2002 by Paul Martin
Illustrations copyright © 2002 by Manu Boisteau Monster Manor
and the Volo colophon are trademarks of Disney Enterprises, Inc.
Volo® is a registered trademark of Disney Enterprises, Inc.
Volo/Hyperion Books for Children are imprints of
Disney Children's Book Group, L.L.C.

All rights reserved. No part of this book may be reproduced or
transmitted in any form or by any means, electronic or mechanical,
including photocopying, recording, or by any information storage and
retrieval system, without written permission from the publisher.

Library of Congress Cataloging-in-Publication Data
This title was previously cataloged with the following information:
Martin, Paul, 1968-
Runaway zombie! / by Paul Martin and Manu Boisteau ;
adapted by Lisa Papademetriou ; illustrated by Manu Boisteau.
p. cm. -- (Monster Manor ; #8)
Summary: Steve and Eye-Gore, the zombies of Monster Manor, are brothers and a
rowdy pair! They listen to loud music and have some strange habits. When Steve is
missing, his brother is convinced he has been zombie-napped. Eye-Gore sets off on a
mission to find Steve and solve the mystery. He ends up uncovering a deep, dark
secret that threatens to destroy all of Monster Manor.
[1. Monsters --Fiction. 2. Brothers --Fiction.]
I. Boisteau, Manu. II. Papademetriou, Lisa. III. Title. IV. Series.
PZ7.M3641833 Run 2003
[FIC]--dc22
2005275750
ISBN 978-1-59961-889-0 (reinforced library bound edition)

All Spotlight books are reinforced library bindings
and manufactured in the United States of America.

Contents

1. Metal Head   1

2. Special Delivery   8

3. All Tied Up   18

4. Zombies in Disguise   25

5. Zombie Rebel   32

6. Crayfish to the Rescue   42

7. A Band on House   49

8. Rescue? What Rescue?   57

9. Chop-Chop!   69

10. Zombificator   75

If you're ever in Transylvaniaville, be sure to stop by Mon Staire Manor. Everyone calls it *Monster* Manor... that's because a bunch of monsters live there.

The Haunted Hills

Nerdburg

Transylvaniaville

Malibu Nightclub

MaLiBU

A Scary-looking Tree

The Slippen Falls

There are lots of fun things to do at the Manor. You can stroll through the cemetery, watch the swamp glow under the moonlight, or make a few new friends!

The FEMUR Family

This sweet little family may look scary, but the truth is that they have no guts at all.

EYE-GORE & STEVE

They want to be skate punks, but they're really just zombies with bad attitudes.

BEATRICE Mon Staire

She's haunted by a horrible secret... and a hairdo that's even worse.

Wolf Man STU

When the moon is full, he becomes human. Well, *somewhat* human...

COUNT SNOBULA

He isn't rich, but he *is* totally stuck up. Thank goodness he sleeps all day.

Created by Von Skalpel,
Frankie is one of a kind.
Thank goodness.

Take a look inside the Manor.
It might be old, but the monsters
think of it as "home, sweet home."

Von Skalpel's
Room

**The Very Dark
Secret Room**

Von Sk
Labor

The
Femur Crypt

Eye-Gore
and
Steve's Pit

The Radioactive Swamp

CHAPTER ONE
Metal Head

The ground of the cemetery behind Mon Staire Manor shook as though it were being torn apart. What was happening? Was it some sort of natural disaster? A hurricane? Flood? Earthquake?

Worse.

The ground was shaking because of the heavy-metal music that was coming from Eye-Gore's crypt.

But no one from the nearby village of

Transylvaniaville dared to complain about the noise. For one thing, there were rumors about Mon Staire Manor. People called it Monster Manor and said that it was haunted by ghosts, witches, werewolves, skeletons, swamp creatures, and more. Naturally, this was completely true. For example, Eye-Gore was a zombie. A real, honest-to-goodness, stinky, ugly zombie. His brother, Steve, was a zombie, too. They were harmless, but they could be very grouchy and looked pretty

scary. Which was why Eye-Gore got to play his music as loudly as he wanted.

Right now, Eye-Gore was listening to his favorite song by his favorite band: "Toothache," by Destructive Poetry. The best thing about the song was that if you played it loudly enough, it actually gave you a toothache.

"Turn it down!" Steve shouted to his brother.

Eye-Gore ignored him and continued looking through the shoe closet. He was searching for a half-eaten pizza he had tossed back there a couple of months ago.

"Ugh!" Eye-Gore said in disgust as he pulled out the piece of pizza, covered with blue mold. "It's still got a fresh spot on it!" He flung the pizza back into the shoe closet, so that it could mold a little longer.

"Eye-Gore!" Steve shouted as he clamped his hands over his ears. The music was so loud that his eyeballs had already vibrated right out of their sockets. "Turn down the music!"

"What?" Eye-Gore shouted. "I can't hear you!" He pointed to the headphones that were clamped over his ears.

Steve shook his head and unplugged the stereo.

"What do you think you're doing?" Eye-Gore screeched. "Don't you know that too much silence can make you go deaf?"

"This is staying unplugged for a week," Steve said, pointing to the stereo. "I'm so sick of your music!"

"You'd better plug that back in," Eye-Gore

said, scowling. "Or else . . ."

"Or else what?" Steve demanded with a smirk.

"Or else your pet is going to be lunch!" Eye-Gore said as he leaped toward the mini-aquarium that was perched on a bureau.

"Leave her alone!" Steve cried, hurrying after Eye-Gore.

Steve had recently taken up a new hobby—raising exotic fish. Unfortunately, Steve was flat broke, so he could afford only a lonely little crayfish, which he had named Soizic.

Soizic was a good little pet—she never complained and seemed perfectly happy in her tank.

Eye-Gore stuck his putrid hand into the water and grabbed Soizic. The little crayfish wiggled her tail. She thought it was time for a walk. Imagine her surprise when Eye-Gore shoved her into his mouth.

"No!" Steve shouted, grabbing his brother by the neck. "Spit her out!"

"Mahk muh," Eye-Gore said, trying to swallow the crayfish.

Steve grabbed Eye-Gore by the feet and flipped him upside down, then gave him a solid whack on the back. Sure enough, Soizic flopped out . . . and so did Eye-Gore's right lung.

Eye-Gore reached for his lung while Steve patted Soizic reassuringly and then placed her gently back in the aquarium.

"You're such a pain, Eye-Gore!" Steve shouted.

"Oh, yeah?" Eye-Gore cried. He thought for a minute. "Same to you!"

But Steve just ignored his brother. "Don't worry, Soizic," he whispered to his little cray-fish. "You're with Daddy now. Everything's going to be all right." And he walked out of the tomb.

Oh, how wrong a zombie can be.

CHAPTER TWO
Special Delivery

*E*ye-Gore sat down to play his favorite video game, Robot Tango. The object of the game was to dance with as many robots as possible without overloading your system. Eye-Gore was pretty good at the game.

Ding-dong!

"Excuse me, Mr. Zombie," someone on the other side of the door said in a hesitant voice, "there is a package for you."

Eye-Gore paused the game and went to

open the front door of the zombies' crypt.

In the doorway stood Frankie, an enormous creature who looked stitched together out of random body parts by someone who didn't really know how to sew. In fact, that's exactly what he was. Frankie was the assistant to Professor Von Skalpel, the Manor's mad scientist. The professor had made Frankie out of body parts he had dug up from the cemetery near the radioactive swamp.

But Frankie wasn't alone. He was holding a mailman under his arm.

"Excuse me," the mailman whimpered, "I've got a package for Steve Zombie, from Liquid Brains on Toast."

Eye-Gore's cold, yellowish heart began to race. Liquid Brains on Toast was Destructive Poetry's record label. Eye-Gore had just ordered the band's latest CD—*Nose Muncher*—

off of the Internet.

"That's a mistake," Eye-Gore said. "The package should be addressed to me—Eye-Gore Zombie."

The mailman hesitated. On the one hand, this zombie was pretty scary-looking. On the other hand, he had taken the sacred Mailperson's Oath: "I will only deliver registered mail to the party named on the package. Photo ID required."

"Sorry," the mailman said after a moment. "This says it's for Steve. I'll need his signature. I can come back tomor—"

"No way, barf brain!" Eye-Gore shouted. "I've gotta have my Destructive Poetry, now!"

Normally, Eye-Gore would have grabbed

the package out of the mailman's hand. But a good mailman was hard to find. Wolf Man Stu usually gobbled them up right away, and then nobody in the Manor got any mail for months. But this one, Herman Crafty, had managed to get away from Stu by spraying himself with dog repellent. Now the mail came regularly. Eye-Gore didn't want to stop getting his heavy-metal magazines on time, so he decided to go easy on the mailman.

"I'll go get Steve," Eye-Gore announced. "Don't let him go, Frankie."

"Aye, aye, Eye-Gore!" Frankie called after the zombie.

Eye-Gore trudged up to the Manor and into the living room. A few of the residents were there, sitting in front of the television. Carlotta Chatter, the TV news anchorwoman for Channel Three, was announcing the latest news in Transylvaniaville.

"Well, it's Environmental Week here in Transylvaniaville," Carlotta chirped. "Oswald B. Smiley, the mayor, tells us about what he has planned for the celebration."

"We aren't letting any toxic clouds into the village for an entire week," the mayor announced. "Also, I've asked Mr. Kleenit, the director of our antipollution efforts, to write a report on the most polluted areas in our town." Mr. Smiley gestured to a rosy-cheeked man standing next to him. "I'll announce the results at the end of the week."

"Sounds like big fun!" Carlotta exclaimed. "And now, on to the annual Most Beautiful Cauliflower contest! It looks like there's a lot of competition this year—"

"Hey, everyone!" Eye-Gore shouted as he ran into the room and stood in front of the TV.

"Has anyone seen Steve?"

"Ugh, no," said Beatrice Mon Staire, the owner of the Manor. She held her nose, and added, "although I think we'd probably smell him before we saw him."

"I don't zink zat he has been here lately," added Professor Von Skalpel in his weird accent.

"Maybe the mayor arrested him," Wolf Man Stu suggested. "He probably thought that he was a toxic cloud!"

"Um, excuse me, Eye-Gore," said a very

large and very green blob of slime.

"Yes, Horror?" Eye-Gore asked eagerly, "have you seen Steve?"

"Er, no," said the shy swamp creature. "I was just wondering if you could move a little to your left. I really want to see who won the cauliflower contest."

Eye-Gore walked out of the Manor grumbling.

"Steve hasn't come back?" Eye-Gore asked when he spotted Frankie standing at the entrance to the zombies' crypt. The mailman was still under Frankie's arm.

Frankie!
Be careful with that package!
And just drop the mailman anywhere.

"Not yet," Frankie said. "Maybe he's still playing with his friends in the road."

Eye-Gore frowned. "Friends? Steve doesn't have any friends! Who are you talking about?"

"I don't know," Frankie admitted. "I passed him earlier. He was in the middle of the road, pretending to fight off five guys in white antiradiation suits. I waved at him, and he shouted, 'Help me, Frankie!' But I didn't have time to play with them; I had to go wash my feet."

"Oh, man!" Eye-Gore wailed. "You are such a noodle-brain! That wasn't a game, Frankie—someone has kidnapped Steve!"

"But why would anyone kidnap Steve?" Frankie asked.

"I don't know! Who *would* want him?" Eye-Gore asked. He shook his head. "I can't believe the only person who saw him get taken away did nothing because he had to go wash his feet!"

"I always do it once a month!" Frankie said defensively.

"Okay, think hard," Eye-Gore commanded. "I know it isn't easy, but try. Did you notice anything else? Anything about the men that might be a clue as to where they took Steve?"

"Nothing!" Frankie insisted. "Like I said, all I saw was five men in antiradiation suits pushing Steve into a truck with the letters 'GPC' written on the side."

"GPC!" Eye-Gore cried. "I should have known!" GPC was short for General Pollution Corporation, Inc., the nearby company that clouded the sky with smoke, morning, noon, and night. It was run by a mean and poorly dressed man named D. K. Pitt, who had once tried to steal the Manor from Beatrice and clean up Horror's beautiful, slimy swamp.

But why would he kidnap Steve? What could the head of an enormous corporation possibly want with a zombie?

CHAPTER THREE
All Tied Up

Steve woke up because something was scratching him on the arm. It was kind of annoying, actually.

"Ugh," Steve said with a groan. He did not feel well. "Where am I?"

He looked around and saw that he was in a small, cozy room.

"Gross!" Steve shouted in disgust. "I've been lying on a soft rug!" He looked around, hoping to see some mold or mildew—even a speck of dirt would have been comforting. But it was no use—the room was perfectly clean. "This is horrible!" Steve moaned. "I've got to get back to my damp, smelly tomb!" Now that Steve was awake, he knew that he was nowhere near the Manor or his messy crypt. He remembered his kidnapping.

Steve tried to move toward the door. But it was no use. Someone had tied Steve up with thick ropes. He couldn't move.

"This is horrible," Steve wailed again. "I've been kidnapped by weird guys in white suits, I'm tied up in a disgustingly clean room, and my arm itches!" Steve wriggled his eyeball at the end of its stalk, and finally managed to look behind his head. A small creature gazed up at him.

"Soizic!" Steve cried happily. He was surprised to see that his pet seemed calm. "My brave little crayfish!"

When the men from GPC tossed Steve into the back of their white van, the zombie had hidden his pet deep in his pocket. When the men took Steve from the van into this room, Soizic had escaped from his pocket and had started trying to claw through the rope that tied Steve to the wall.

"Good thinking, Soizic!" Steve cheered. "My crayfish is a genius!"

While it was true that Soizic's intelligence was way above average for a crustacean, Soizic's escape plan wasn't really as brilliant as it might have seemed. For one thing, her claws were about a half an inch long. For another, the rope she was trying to saw through was as thick as a banana. At Soizic's current rate, it would have taken her roughly 113 years to saw through the rope . . . with no time for lunch breaks.

After twenty minutes of watching Soizic saw away at the rope, Steve realized that his pet looked pretty tired.

"Stop, Soizic, stop!" Steve begged. "You've been out of water for too long. Your shell is going to crack!" It was a well-known fact that crayfish needed to be in water or else their shells cracked—which wasn't a pretty sight. He looked around for a puddle or a damp spot—but the room was perfectly clean and completely dry.

"Poor girl!" Steve cried. "You're trying to help me, but you're drying out like a stick of old chewing gum. I should have let Eye-Gore swallow you. . . ."

Suddenly, Steve got quiet. He had a brilliant idea. . . .

"Okay, Sleeping Beauty," one of the men in the white suits said to Steve as he opened the door to the room. "It's time to see the boss."

Steve didn't bother to reply.

Another man appeared, and the two grunted as they hoisted Steve onto a stretcher. The gurney squeaked as it rolled down the hall, which was lined with rusty pipes.

Where am I? Steve wondered as he heard the slow drip of thick liquid through the pipes. Those pipes sound like the tide of the radioactive swamp under a full moon, he thought, and he became homesick.

Finally, the men wheeled Steve into a large room filled with cans bearing the GPC logo. So he wasn't that surprised when he heard

D. K. Pitt's voice ring out in the room.

"Welcome, Mr. Zombie," Pitt said with an evil grin. "How nice of you to drop by, even though you were all tied up." Pitt laughed at his joke. Steve did not.

The two men hauled Steve into a chair as Pitt crossed the room to stand behind a computer that was perched on a high table.

He looks even fatter and balder than he did when he tried to destroy

Horror's swamp, Steve thought. And he looks even meaner, which seemed impossible.

"Do you have anything to say before I begin my experiment?" Pitt asked.

Steve shook his head. What could he say? After all, his mouth was full of crayfish—Soizic, to be specific.

"Outstanding!" Pitt cried. He punched a few buttons on the keyboard and let out an evil laugh.

A long tube descended from the ceiling and came to a stop barely an inch from Steve's face. The zombie stared at the tube and frowned. Wow, Steve thought, if I wasn't already dead, I think I'd be pretty worried about this. . . .

CHAPTER FOUR
Zombies in Disguise

Back at the Manor, Eye-Gore knew what he had to do. "I have to save Steve!" he cried. "And his little crayfish, too!" But how? General Pollution Corporation was all the way on the other side of Deadwood Forest and the Haunted Hills. It was a long trip for a zombie.

"My legs will fall off before I go half a mile," Eye-Gore said to himself.

"Um, can I get down now?" Herman Crafty

asked Frankie, who still had the mailman tucked under his arm. "I need to deliver a few more letters today."

"How can I get there?" Eye-Gore wondered aloud. "How? How? How?" He tapped himself on the forehead so hard that one of his eye-balls fell out and rolled away. It came to a stop right beside the back wheel of Herman Crafty's bicycle.

"Holy Tamales!" Eye-Gore cried. "That's just what I need!" He ran over, picked up the eye, popped it back into place, and hopped onto the bike.

"Hey!" the mailman shouted after him. "That's my bike! It's government property!"

But the zombie was already pedaling down the road. "I promise I'll give it back." Eye-Gore shouted. "Frankie! Give the mailman a lift anywhere he needs to go!"

"Sure thing!" Frankie shouted, waving. "Have a nice ride!" Frankie looked down at the mailman. "Now—where to?"

Eye-Gore passed through the countryside surrounding Transylvaniaville and soon emerged into a soot-colored landscape of dead grass and dried-out bushes. Two tall chimneys coughed smoke into the air. Low buildings and rusty tanks half-eaten by acid led up to the GPC factory itself. Eye-Gore squeezed his brakes and stepped off the bicycle at a spot near the entrance.

How can I get inside? Eye-Gore wondered, staring at the plant. And once I get inside, how will I find Steve? I'll never blend in with those humans. They'll know I'm a zombie right away.

The truth was, Eye-Gore had hardly ever

left the cemetery before this outing. Everything he knew about the human world came from video games, music videos, songs, and movies.

"I guess I could build a tunnel under the factory," Eye-Gore said to himself. He had seen that done in a movie called *Born To Dig*. The hero had dug a tunnel to rescue his best friend from prison. But it had taken the man thirty years to dig the tunnel, and by the time he got inside, his best friend had announced that he was having a great time in jail and

This place is gorgeous!

didn't want to leave. "It would take too long, anyway," Eye-Gore grumbled in frustration.

"Could I hide in a soda machine?" Eye-Gore wondered, spotting one near the factory entrance. The plan had potential . . . although he couldn't imagine what people would think if they saw a soda machine wandering around the factory. "Someone might get suspicious," the zombie decided after some thought.

Suddenly, Eye-Gore heard the sound of tires on gravel. He hid behind a drum of toxic waste as a green truck with *Transylvaniaville Pollution Control* written on the side pulled to a stop. A man got out and began to step into a green protection suit. Eye-Gore thought the man looked vaguely familiar.

"I know! It's that guy from TV," Eye-Gore said to himself. "Mr. Kleenit—the antipollution dude."

As Mr. Kleenit struggled with the zipper on the front of his protection suit, Eye-Gore grabbed the biggest rock he could find. The zombie crept up behind Kleenit without making a sound. "I'll knock him out cold and take his protection suit," Eye-Gore said softly to himself. With one quick motion, Eye-Gore hurled the rock at Kleenit's head.

"Ouch!" Kleenit cried, rubbing his head. "What was that?"

Um, did I forget to mention that the biggest rock that Eye-Gore could find was roughly the size of an M&M?

The antipollution director turned to see where the little rock had come from. His face held a mixture of confusion and annoyance. That is, until he saw Eye-Gore.

"*Aiiiiiiieeeeeee!*" Kleenit screeched at the sight of the zombie. Then, he fainted.

"Hmmm," Eye-Gore said as he stared down at Kleenit. "Well, that was easy."

Eye-Gore slipped on Kleenit's protective suit. Then he lifted the human into the truck and tried to make him as comfortable as possible. "I promise I'll give the suit back as soon as I find Steve," Eye-Gore whispered to the director. He did feel slightly guilty about stealing the suit.

The zombie, decked out in his new outfit, walked toward the factory to save his brother.

Thanks for the loan, Kleenit!

CHAPTER FIVE:
Zombie Rebel

"Good morning, and welcome to GPC," the receptionist said as Eye-Gore walked in through the front door. "Do you have an appointment?" She didn't even bat an eyelash at the zombie—after all, his face was completely hidden by the protection suit.

"Uh—good morning," Eye-Gore said in his most official-sounding voice. "I'm the antipollution dude. I'm here for a tour-thingie of this factory-type deal."

The receptionist's fingers flew across her keyboard as she peered at her computer. "I'm sorry, Mr. Kleenit, but the man in charge of toxic waste is on vacation. I can make another appointment for you. How does four P.M. on April 12, 2047, sound?"

"Well, I am free that day," Eye-Gore admitted. But then he stopped himself. Wait a minute, he thought. I can't wait around for over forty years to free my brother! Eye-Gore gritted his teeth. What would U. R. Anut, the lead singer of Destructive Poetry, have said in such a situation?

Suddenly, the words to Eye-Gore's favorite song flooded into his head, and he hollered:

I am a rebel! A loose-toothed rebel!
I howl like a dog, I bite like a cat,
I sing like a platypus,

What do you think about that?

The receptionist's eyes grew wide, and she pressed a red button.

I think my singing really impressed her, Eye-Gore thought as he folded his arms across his chest and nodded at the receptionist. That must be the "important guy" button, he decided.

Meanwhile, Steve, still strapped to his seat inside the factory, heard the alarm start to blare. The steel doors on the other side of the room clanged shut and a red light began to flash.

Wanh! Wanh! Wanh! screamed the alarm.

That sounds like one of Eye-Gore's favorite songs, Steve thought, suddenly missing his brother.

"What do you think of my little alarm sys-

tem?" Pitt asked Steve. He was leering at the young zombie in his evil-dude way.

Steve didn't bother answering. He was way too tired. For the past hour, Pitt had smeared different ointments and creams over half of Steve's face. Steve barely had the energy to wonder what the man was doing to him. Besides, there wasn't a mirror in sight.

Suddenly, the alarm went quiet and the

huge, steel doors slid open. Two GPC men dragged in a figure wearing a green protection suit.

"Boss," one of the men said to Pitt, "this guy claims to be the director of pollution control."

"*I howl at the wind, I'm a flat-faced rebel!*" the figure in the green suit screamed.

Steve smiled. He knew those words.

"Mr. Kleenit!" Pitt cried, thinking that Eye-Gore really was the antipollution dude. "What are you doing?—I mean— What a wonderful surprise! Guards, release this man." Pitt waved the guards away.

The two GPC men released Eye-Gore.

"Holy Pepperoni!" Eye-Gore shouted at Pitt when he caught sight of his brother. "What have you done to his face?"

Half of Steve's face was just as it had been

before—covered with rotting flesh. But the other half . . . had skin as pink and smooth as a baby's.

"No, no, you don't understand," Pitt said smoothly. "I've fixed this man's skin with my new beauty product—"

Just then, Steve opened his mouth, and a pink torpedo launched itself at Pitt's face.

"Yikes!" Pitt cried. "Get this crazy crayfish off of me!"

Soizic, who was feeling much better after spending a lot of time in Steve's mouth, pinched Pitt's left nostril hard.

"Yeow!" Pitt shouted.

Eye-Gore hurried toward the computer and started punching buttons at random in an attempt to release his brother. Unfortunately, his efforts set off the sprinkler system, turned up the central heating unit, and blasted elevator music throughout the building before he finally managed to set Steve free.

"Get this monster off me!" Pitt cried again as he staggered across the room. "I'm allergic to shellfish!" Soizic pinched harder, and Pitt turned green, then fainted onto the floor.

Eye-Gore peeled off his protective mask. "Let's get out of here!" he shouted.

Steve grabbed Soizic, and the two zombies took off.

"*Mummph* . . ." Pitt murmured. He put a hand to his head and sat up. "They're gone!" he cried, looking around. "I have to stop them before they tell anyone!"

He hurried to the computer, jabbed at a button, and grabbed the microphone. "Attention! Attention!" he cried. "Two dangerous men with green skin and horrible body odor are trying to escape. Stop them at all costs!"

"Quick!" Eye-Gore cried as they reached Herman Crafty's bicycle. "Jump on the rack in the back, and I'll pedal."

"But the rack's uncomfortable," Steve said in a whiny tone.

"Fine, I'll go on the rack," Eye-Gore said.

"You want me to do all of the pedaling?" Steve complained. "In this heat?"

Eye-Gore rolled his eyes, one of which actually tried to roll away altogether. Luckily, he caught it in time. "Why did I come here to save you?" he groaned. "I should have let them make all of your skin baby-soft!"

"That's a horrible thing to say!" Steve shouted.

Suddenly, they heard cries. "There they are!"

Steve and Eye-Gore looked over and saw two GPC men running toward them.

"Oh, great!" Eye-Gore shouted. "Now it's too late!"

Steve looked around. To the right was the road—but everyone would see where they went if they took that route. To the left was a very nasty-looking river.

I am not getting in that sludge water, Steve thought. To the rear was an abandoned house. . . .

"Quick, into the house!" Steve shouted.

But Eye-Gore was one step ahead of him. He yanked open the worm-eaten door and gestured for his brother to move inside.

"Just a minute!" Steve said suddenly. "I'm going to send an SOS!"

CHAPTER SIX
Crayfish to the Rescue

"Hello, little buddy," Horror said, when the tiny crayfish paddled up to him. "You've never come around here before." Horror had been peacefully paddling around the radioactive swamp, taking his weekly bath, when Soizic had appeared in front of him, looking worn out and desperate.

Horror picked the crayfish up and tried to play with her, but it became apparent that the crustacean was in no mood for games.

"Hmmm," Horror said, inspecting Soizic closely, "I wonder what's wrong." After a few moments, he found the problem. There was a piece of paper wrapped around the crayfish's neck. Horror pulled the paper off her and unfolded it. But it took him several minutes to understand the message.

For one thing, the zombies were horrible spellers.

For another thing, Horror hadn't even realized that Steve and Eye-Gore were missing. Sure, the Femur family had noticed that Eye-Gore wasn't playing his Destructive Poetry CD at his usual brain-liquifying volume, but they'd just figured that Steve had stolen the CD and hidden it. They were happy not to hear that music all day long. And Frankie had taken off carrying the mailman through Transylvaniaville to deliver the rest of his packages, so he hadn't had a chance to mention anything to anyone. That was why it took Horror a while to understand the message brought by the crayfish.

"Everyone!" Horror cried as he burst into the Manor a few moments later. "This is an emergency! The Zombies need our help!"

Wolf Man Stu, the Femurs, Beatrice, Professor Von Skalpel, and Count Snobula didn't even look up from the documentary

they were watching. "Shhh, Horror," Count Snobula said. "You've arrived just in time to hear about the elephant slug—the largest slug in the world."

"Oh, that does sound interesting," Horror said, turning toward the TV. Then he shook his head. "But I just got an SOS from the Zombies!"

"Horror," Beatrice said, rolling her eyes, "would you please wipe your feet on the doormat before squishing through the whole house?"

Horror's right. I think I'll make a little butter sauce for crayfish dip.

"Sorry." Horror hurried to the front door and wiped his feet, then jogged back to the living room with a quick *splatsplatsplat*. Everyone had turned back toward the TV.

"Doesn't anyone want to

read the message?" Horror wailed.

"I vill look at it," the professor said. "Hand it over."

Dear Evrybody,
HELP! We are trapd in an a band on house!

"Hee-hee!" The scientist giggled after reading the first sentence out loud. "A band on! Zey cannot even schpell *abandoned!*" He shook his head and kept reading the letter out loud.

It's nere the GPC faktory. Thear r a bunch of men hoo want to kidnap us and putt creme on us. Come qwik!
Sined,
Your friends Eye-Gore and Steve
P.S.: This is not a jocke. Can yu please fead my crayfish? Thank yu.

"Ha-ha-ha!" Von Skalpel cracked up. "Zose crazy zombies—vhere on earth did zey learn to schpell?"

Horror rolled his eyes. "So? Are we going to help them?"

The monsters blinked up at Horror.

"The world's largest slug can weigh fifteen pounds," the voice from the TV announced.

Wolf Man Stu coughed uncomfortably. "Look, Horror, those two doofuses didn't help me when the villagers of Transylvaniaville thought I was taking all the sheep. Why should I help them?"

"Yes, and they shouldn't be near GPC, anyway," Snobula pointed out quite snobbily.

"They alwayth play their muthic too loud," Bonehead lisped. "It'th annoying."

"Yes, and they have terrible attitudes," Beatrice added.

"But Steve and Eye-Gore *need* help!" Horror wailed. "What are we going to do?"

"I have an idea!" Fibula Femur announced. "Let's reorganize their tomb and use it as a game room!"

"Yippee!" shouted Bonehead and Kneecap cheerfully. "We finally have a plan!"

CHAPTER SEVEN
A Band on House

Night had fallen. The wind rustled in the trees. Crickets chirped. And four men from GPC were beating on the door to an abandoned house, while two zombies tried to keep them out.

"Steve! Help me move this cupboard in front of the door!" Eye-Gore shouted.

"I can't!" Steve shouted as he shoved his back against the worm-eaten door. "If I move, they'll bust through!"

As he said that, one of the GPC men hurled a rock through the glass panel at the top of the rear door. The glass shattered with a loud crash. Quickly, Eye-Gore yanked the cupboard and put all his weight behind it. Then with a mighty heave, he hauled the enormous antique in front of the rear door.

"Ooof!" cried the man who had thrown the rock. He had tried to hurl himself through the rear door but ended up slamming headfirst into the cupboard.

"One down!" Eye-Gore shouted.

Steve picked up a board and quickly nailed it across the door. "This will keep them out for a few minutes—but they'll get through eventually. We need to find something to keep them away. Something that humans hate."

"Fire?" Eye-Gore suggested.

Steve rolled his eyeballs. "Okay, something

that humans hate, and zombies don't hate," he clarified.

"Ice water?"

"Not good enough."

"Doughnuts?"

"What planet are you from?" Steve demanded.

Eye-Gore looked around. They didn't have much to work with. Finally, his eyes came back to rest on the cupboard.

"I know!" Eye-Gore cried. With a lightning-quick move, he grabbed a plate and a fork from the cupboard. He scratched the fork slowly across the plate, producing a horrible *skreek!*

"Aaargh!" The GPC men outside fell to the

ground and covered their ears.

Even Steve, who didn't really have ears, shuddered. "Good work, Eye-Gore. Let me help you out!"

The zombie hurried toward the cupboard for another plate and fork. Suddenly, Steve noticed something on the floor. He peered at it closely. "Eye-Gore, did you bring any of your CDs here?"

"No," Eye-Gore said, still scratching away. "Why?"

Steve pointed to three CDs that were lying on the floor. They were all by Destructive Poetry.

"Wow, the people who used to live here sure had great taste," Eye-Gore said.

Thunk! Thunk! Thunk!

One of the GPC men was using an ax to try to chop down the door.

The zombies turned back to their plates and scratched hard enough to make a bald man grow hair.

"Look!" Steve shouted as he stared out the window, "They're running!"

It was true. The GPC men were hurrying back toward the factory.

Eye-Gore had stopped scratching and opened the top drawer of a nearby bureau. "Steve," he said softly, "you're number one."

"You bet I'm number one!" Steve shouted.

"Get lost, GPC losers!" he hollered out the window.

"That's not what I meant," Eye-Gore said. He shook his head and held out two small plastic badges. "Look."

Steve looked down at the ID cards. The one on the left showed a picture of a heavyset young guy. At the top, in bold letters, was printed GPC, and underneath was a name and a number: STEVE SWEET, 0001. The card on the right had a picture of a skinny guy who looked oddly familiar. IGOR SWEET, 0002, the tag read.

"That's us," Steve said. "That's us before we became zombies. I understand everything now."

"Wow," Eye-Gore said, nodding. "Um, would you mind explaining it?"

"We were the first two workers at GPC," Steve said, looking around the house. "And this was where we lived. We must have had an accident with the deadly chemicals at the plant. . . ."

". . . And the chemicals turned us into zombies," Eye-Gore finished.

"Pitt must have tried to bury us in the closest cemetery," Steve added.

"Behind the Manor!" Eye-Gore realized. "But we weren't dead. . . . We were undead."

"We woke up and didn't remember anything, which made us grouchy, which is why we're zombies with bad attitudes!" Steve cried.

"It all makes sense!" Eye-Gore said.

Thud! Thud! Thud!

The GPC men were back—with an even bigger ax!

Steve and Eye-Gore scratched away at their plates, letting out a loud and painful symphony of *screeeee*s.

"It isn't working!" Eye-Gore shouted. "They must be wearing earplugs!"

The two zombies worked together to shove a musty old couch in front of the door.

"Don't worry, Eye-Gore," Steve said to his brother. "By now, our friends will definitely be on the way to rescue us."

CHAPTER EIGHT
Rescue? What Rescue?

"**W**hoo-hoo!" Bonehead shouted as his father opened the door to the zombies' crypt. "Thith ith going to be a thpectacular game room! With a ping-pong table!"

"Ugh," said his sister, Kneecap. "This place is disgusting!"

"Look!" Bonehead called. He was standing in front of the television in the corner. "There'th already a bunch of video gamth!"

"You put those down!" his mother, Tibia

Femur, commanded. "No son of mine is going to play some zombie's horribly violent video games!"

"Yeah, kids, don't touch anything," Fibula added. "Who knows what those zombies have lying around."

"Look! Thtairth!" Bonehead said, opening a doorway to a ladder that led down into another room. He hurried down the steps.

"Be careful!" his mother called, clacking down the stairs after him.

But it was too late. Bonehead was never good at being careful. For example, right now, he stood on a rickety chair on top of a three-legged table trying to reach something on a high shelf of the zombies' pantry.

"Oooh! Yogurt!" Bonehead said as he grabbed a carton from the top shelf.

"No-o-o-o-o-o!" his mother screamed.

But it was too late. Bonehead pulled open the lid before checking the expiration date—which was July 7, 1956. The food was a time bomb that had silently ticked away, forgotten in the back of the pantry, biding its time.

The stench had barely escaped from under the lid when it knocked Bonehead to the floor at a single whiff. His skull popped off when he hit the ground.

"My baby!" Tibia screeched as she ran toward her son—but in that moment, the awful smell reached her and knocked her out, too.

"What's going on?" Fibula screamed from the top of the stairs. When there was no reply, he clattered halfway down the steps. One look at his wife and son on the floor next to the opened yogurt container told him every-thing he needed to know. There was nothing he could do for Bonehead or Tibia—Fibula had to save himself and his daughter. He raced back upstairs and shut the door before the noxious fumes could follow him. Still, a bit of the scent escaped under the door.

Fibula gagged, then picked up Kneecap and ran.

"Help!" Fibula shouted as he ran toward the Manor at top speed. "Chemical alert!"

Hearing the frantic shouts,

Swamp Horror and Frankie burst out of the house.

"What's wrong?" Horror asked. "Are the zombies back?"

"No!" Fibula shouted. "Their yogurt is attacking!" He explained about the nauseating stench.

"Awful smells have never bothered me," Horror said. "I'll go get them." He took three steps toward the zombies' crypt and stopped. Suddenly, he turned an even more vibrant shade of green and fell over with a horrible *splat*.

"Oh, no," Fibula cried. "If Horror can't stand the smell, who can?"

Frankie sniffed. "I think the stink is getting closer."

It was true. The wind was rustling through the trees, carrying the awful stench toward the Manor.

"All right," Wolf Man Stu said as he looked around the living room suspiciously. "Who's responsible for that smell?"

"Oh, no!" Count Snobula said in an outraged tone. "Has Frankie been eating beans again?"

"It was the zombies' fault!" Fibula shouted as he ran into the living room. "With all of their rancid food, this was bound to happen! Their yogurt has knocked Tibia and Bonehead out cold."

"I see," Professor Von Skalpel said, stroking

his beard. "I should have known—zis schtench
could only be zee schtench of outdated yogurt.
I zink I have an idea. Frankie, follow me."

Von Skalpel and Frankie bustled into the
laboratory, and, a minute later, they came out,
each wearing enormous face masks and carrying another. Frankie also had a large white
laundry bag over his shoulder.

"Poo bis glon gloor glase," the professor

said as he handed Fibula a mask. It was impossible to understand Von Skalpel through the mask.

"What was that?" Fibula asked.

"Poo bis glon gloor glase!" the professor repeated, speaking louder and motioning to Fibula to put on the mask.

"I have no idea what you're saying," Fibula said. "So I'm just going to put this on my face."

Von Skalpel, Fibula, and Frankie headed out to the zombies' crypt. Fibula showed them to the stairs that led to the cellar. The professor paused when he saw the foul green air seeping under the cellar door, and motioned for Frankie to go first. The professor followed.

"Glun!" the professor said a moment later, as he leaped up the stairs, taking them three at a time.

Fibula wasn't sure what the professor had said, but he knew he'd better run. He tore out of the crypt, with the professor and Frankie only a little bit behind him. The professor was staggering from the stench, in spite of his mask.

Von Skalpel didn't take the mask off until he reached the Manor. "It vas horrible!" he cried. "Zee yogurt tried to melt my brain by going in zrough my ears!"

"What about Bonehead and Tibia?" Fibula cried, catching up to him. "Did you find them?"

Your family, Mr. Femur!

"Zort of," the professor admitted.

Frankie stepped forward and emptied the contents of the white laundry bag. Bones spilled out all over the floor.

"Do you like puzzles?" Von Skalpel asked. He watched Fibula hopefully as Bonehead's and Tibia's skulls rolled toward the front door.

"Whee!" Bonehead shouted as his head rolled away.

"Ow!" Tibia cried. "Try to be a little more careful!"

"They're awake!" Fibula shouted. "Don't worry, we'll have you back together in no time."

"All we need are all the king's horses and all the king's men," Beatrice said as she walked into the front hall, holding her nose. "Look, I'm glad the Femur family is back together, but what are we going to do about that horrible smell? It's just disgusting!"

At that moment, Horror staggered inside. "I think the wind has changed," he said hopefully.

"But zat von't last forever," the professor pointed out. "I don't zink any vun of us should risk going out zere again. Zat yogurt is powerful and angry. In fact, I zink only zee zombies can put up viz zee smell long enough to destroy zee yogurt."

"Then what are we waiting for?" Horror demanded. "Let's go save them!"

The professor sighed. "But how vill vee get all zee vay to zee GPC factory?" he asked.

"Right," Beatrice added. "None of us has a car."

Beep! Beep!

Just then, Herman Crafty pulled up to the Manor's front gate. He was driving a brand-new, souped-up mail truck. He had demanded that he be allowed to use the supervisor's truck until his bicycle was replaced.

Beep! Beep! The proud little postman honked his horn to announce the mail.

"Problem solved," Beatrice said.

CHAPTER NINE
Chop-Chop!

"This is not going well!" Steve shouted as he shoved his shoulder against a desk.

The men from GPC were back, and not only did they have earplugs, they had axes and crowbars. They had already torn down the front door and were now busy hacking through the teacher's desk pushed up behind it.

"Once they're through the desk, they'll be able to chop through the sofa and the cupboard. Then we're done for!" Steve shouted.

"Eye-Gore, get us some more furniture!"

"There isn't any more furniture!" Eye-Gore wailed. "Just some tasteful, red, throw pillows!"

"What are we going to do?" Steve shouted.

"Wait!" Eye-Gore cried. "I have an idea!"

Steve used all his strength to push against the pile of furniture separating him and his brother from the men chopping outside.

There was a huge, creaking groan, and then Eye-Gore appeared with some large planks. "Quick, help me!" he shouted as he started to nail the planks into place over the already chopped-up door.

"This is great!" Steve shouted as he held the planks for Eye-Gore. "Where did you get all of this wood?"

Eye-Gore jerked his head toward the rear of the room, but kept hammering. "Back

there," he said, impatiently.

Steve turned to see a huge, gaping wall in the back of the house. Through it was a lovely view of the countryside, with a babbling brook, and a few cows. But Steve didn't have time to admire the scenery.

"Eye-Gore, you idiot!" Steve shouted. "Now they can get in through the back!"

Eye-Gore frowned and turned to look at the hole. "Gosh," he said, "I didn't think of that!"

A moment later, there was a horrible roar,

71

and then a very loud shout:

"Attack!"

"Not from zat direction! From zee left! Zee left!"

Splat! Splat! Splat!

Steve crawled under the desk while Eye-Gore tried to hide behind the sofa. An enormous shadow appeared at the hole in the rear wall.

"Mister Eye-Gore?" the shadow asked politely. "Mister Steve? Your rescue team is here."

"Frankie! Ow!" Steve shouted, because—once he realized who was at the rear of the house—he had jumped up and knocked his head on the desk.

Frankie turned and shouted, "I've got them!"

A cheer went up from outside.

"Where are all the GPC guys?" Eye-Gore

asked, still hiding behind the sofa.

"They ran off!" Swamp Horror said, as he, the professor, and all of the other monsters hurried up behind Frankie. "All we did was drive up and scream, and they freaked out!"

"Well, you did throw a little slime at a couple of them," Wolf Man Stu added.

"True," Horror admitted. "Do you think it was too much?"

"Oh, no," Stu replied. "I thought it was a nice touch."

"But, wait," Steve said. "I have one question—where's Soizic?"

"She's right here!" Horror cried, pulling

out a jar full of green, slimy water. The heroic little crayfish was paddling happily around inside.

Soizic leaped out of her jar and jumped onto Steve's cheek. She rubbed her claws against his decomposing face.

"That's so beautiful!" Frankie said, his eyes filling with tears. "I'm so glad that this story has a happy ending. And now, you can come home with us and destroy the horrible yog—"

"Not so fast!" shouted a voice.

The monsters turned to see D. K. Pitt standing before them. He was holding a tube with the word ZOMBIFICATOR printed on the side.

"You'll all kindly back out of the room and follow me," Pitt said with an evil laugh. "Because if you don't—I'll turn everyone in Transylvaniaville into a zombie!"

CHAPTER TEN
Zombificator

"That would be awesome!" Eye-Gore said excitedly.

The others turned to stare at him.

"For me, personally, I mean," Eye-Gore explained.

The others continued to stare. It didn't stop him.

"Because then, I'd have a lot of zombies to hang out with—"

"Silence!" Pitt shouted. "Let's go, zombies.

Follow me—I still need you!"

"Why should we do what you say?" Steve demanded, scowling at Pitt. "Eye-Gore and I aren't afraid of your thingamajig. We already are zombies!"

"But your friends aren't," Pitt said, aiming the tube at the other monsters. "Not yet."

"Okay, they'll go with you," Wolf Man Stu said quickly, shoving Steve toward Pitt. The wolf man had no intention of being purified.

"What are you going to do?" Steve wailed. "Put more cream on us?"

"Of course he is, you fool!" Professor Von Skalpel shouted. "Do you not get it? He is going to test his face cream on you. Vunce it vorks, he vill schpray a cloud of Zombificator over Transylvaniaville. Zee villagers vill be horrible, stinking, hideous zombies—"

"Hey!" Eye-Gore said, hurt. "Be nice!"

"No—your professor is right," Pitt said. "When the villagers are zombies, they'll have to buy my skin cream to get back to normal. I'll make the price sky high—and then I'll be rich!"

"Unless I shut you down, Mr. Pitt," said a voice.

Pitt turned to see a tiny figure standing behind him.

"Look! It's Mr. Kleenit—the antipollution

director!" Eye-Gore shouted. "Um . . . hey, sorry about earlier," he added.

Kleenit waved his hand. "Hitting me with a pebble is a small crime compared to the one I've just heard described. Mr. Pitt, I'm arresting you for attempted zombification of an entire town. Drop your weapon and follow me."

"Never!" Pitt shouted. "I'll use it on you first!"

Pitt aimed the tube at Kleenit. But before he could pull the trigger, he let out a scream of pain.

"Go, Soizic!" Steve shouted.

The brave little crayfish had jumped onto Pitt's shirt and clamped the tip of his ear in her pincers, hard.

"No, no!" Pitt screeched. "Stop it! Have pity on me!"

Pitt whacked at Soizic with the tube of Zombificator. But the little crayfish was just too fast—with a leap, she hurled herself into Steve's arms just as the tube started to hiss. Pitt had pulled the trigger!

"No!" Pitt shouted again, as a dark cloud surrounded him.

The monsters didn't wait around to see what happened next. They piled out of the house with Kleenit right behind them, still taking notes in his notebook.

Von Skalpel leaped behind the wheel of the new mail truck and started the engine.

"And now, let's take on that yogurt!"

Horror shouted as the mail truck roared toward the Manor.

"Yogurt?" Steve said as his stomach let out a low growl. "Man, that sounds good. I think I still have some in the pantry. . . ."

And so, everything ended well.

Steve scarfed down the yogurt the minute he got home, which not only got rid of the horrible smell around the Manor, but turned the half of his face that had gone baby-smooth back to its normal, greenish color. And, although the zombies went back to fighting after a few days, Eye-Gore never tried to swallow Soizic again.

Kneecap, Beatrice, and Fibula had fun putting Bonehead and Tibia back together. It only took three days.

Horror threw a party out at the swamp to

celebrate the victories over Mr. Pitt and the yogurt. The zombies offered to bring milk products, but Horror insisted that they leave those at home.

And Mr. D. K. Pitt? Well, once he disappeared into the smog created by his Zombificator, no one ever saw him again. Some people said that he had run off with tons of money from GPC, but others told a very different tale. After all, it wasn't long after his mysterious disappearance that the villagers of Transylvaniaville stopped going near the abandoned house next to the GPC factory.

They say that a horrible monster lives there—one who is even more terrifying than the ones who live in Monster Manor.